THIS BOOK BELONGS TO:

_____

This paperback edition first published in 2011 by Andersen Press Ltd.

First published in Great Britain in 1991 by Andersen Press Ltd.,

20 Vauxhall Bridge Road, London SW1V 2SA.

Copyright © Tony Ross, 1991

The rights of Tony Ross to be identified as the author and illustrator

of this work have been asserted by him in accordance with

the Copyright, Designs and Patents Act, 1988.

All rights reserved. Colour separated in Switzerland by Photolitho AG, Zürich.

Printed and bound in China by Toppan Leefung.

10   9   8   7

British Library Cataloguing in Publication Data available.

ISBN 978 1 84270 936 8

This book has been printed on acid-free paper

DON'T DO THAT!

TONY ROSS

ANDERSEN PRESS

Nellie had a pretty nose.

It was so pretty that it won pretty nose competitions.

It was so pretty that Nellie was given a part in the Christmas play, with Donna and Patricia, who had pretty noses too.

"CHILDREN, don't do that!" said her teacher.

"It won't come out, sir," said Nellie. "It's *stuck.*"

The teacher tried to get Nellie's finger out, but he couldn't.

Neither could the head teacher.
"It's stuck," they said, and sent Nellie home.

"It's stuck," said Nellie.
"I can get it out," said Henry.
"Mum," shouted Nellie.

But Mum couldn't get Nellie's finger out.
"I can," said Henry.

So Mum called the doctor.
"I can't get it out," he said.
"I can," said Henry.

So the doctor called the police.
"We can't get it out," they said.
"I can," said Henry.

So the police called the conjurer.
"I can't get it out," he said.
"I can," said Henry.

So the conjurer called the farmer.
"I can't get it out," said the farmer.
"I can," said Henry.

So the farmer called the fire brigade.
"We can't get it out," they said.
"I can," said Henry.

Nobody could get Nellie's finger out.
Her nose was longer, and it hurt.
There was only one thing left to do.

"I can get it out," said Henry.

So everybody called the scientist.
"Of course I can get it out," he said.
"Science can do anything."

And he measured Nellie's nose.
"I can get it out," said Henry.

So the scientist built a rocket ship, and tied it to Nellie's arm.

Then he tied Nellie's leg to the park bench.

Then he set off the rocket . . .

. . . but Nellie's finger *still* wouldn't come out.

"I can get it out," said Henry.

"Go on then!" said the teachers, Mum, the doctor, the police, the conjurer, the farmer, the fire brigade and the scientist.

So Henry tickled Nellie . . .
. . . and it worked!

The
end →

TONY ROSS

Tony Ross was born in London and trained at the Liverpool School of Art. He has worked as a cartoonist, graphic designer, and art director of an advertising agency. He is now considered to be one of the finest contemporary children's illustrators, and his books are published all over the world.

Tony Ross has illustrated over eight hundred books for children, many of which are considered modern classics. His books include: *Tadpole's Promise, I Hate School, Mayfly Day,* and *I'm Coming to Get You!*, as well as the bestselling Little Princess books, which have now been made into an award-winning animated television series.

OTHER BOOKS BY TONY ROSS:

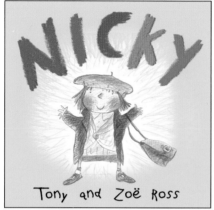

9781842706114

9781842706916

9781842707449

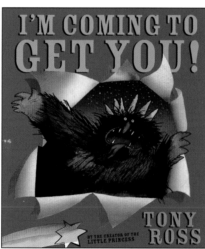

9781842707432

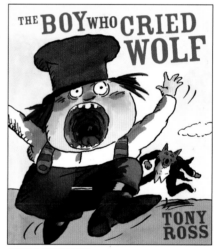

9781842708330

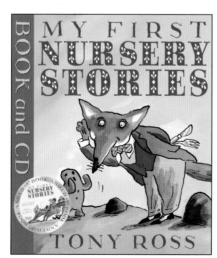

9781842709726

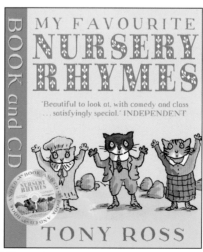

9781842709733